REMEMBRANCE

Books by Alistair MacLeod

The Lost Salt Gift of Blood (1976)

As Birds Bring Forth the Sun (1986)

No Great Mischief (1999)

Island: The Collected Stories (2000)

To Every Thing There Is a Season:
A Cape Breton Christmas Story
(with illustrations by Peter Rankin, 2004, 2012)

Remembrance (2014)

Alistair MacLeod

REMEMBRANCE

A Story

McClelland & Stewart

Library and Archives of Canada Cataloguing in Publication
is available upon request.

ISBN: 978-0-7710-5451-8
ebook ISBN: 978-0-7710-5578-2

Printed and bound in USA

McClelland & Stewart,
a division of Random House of Canada Limited,
a Penguin Random House Company
www.randomhouse.ca

1   2   3   4   5   18   17   16   15   14

REMEMBRANCE

1.

When David MacDonald went out to stand by his woodpile, the sky was still dark, although the grey light of the approaching morning was beginning to make itself known. It would not be the kind of morning associated with the earlier summer when, if one waited long enough, the sun would gradually appear over the mountaintops to the east. Then the night's dew would slowly evaporate, the petals of the flowers would begin to open, and the sounds of the approaching day would replace those of the departing night.

The raucous crows that nested in the trees above his house would begin their squabbling conversations, even as the yelping of the coyote pack, farther to the north, would gradually subside. The squirrels would begin to chatter, and the wasps would begin to tentatively appear from under the eaves of his shed. The deer that grazed in the field above his house would gradually fade into the surrounding forest; he could sense their quiet movements almost more than he could see them.

Because of his deteriorating eyesight, he sometimes mistook the standing spruce trees for deer, straining his eyes to see if the shapes would move. He knew he should visit an eye doctor to test his failing vision but feared that unwelcome results might lead to the cancellation of his driver's licence. Now he rarely drove at night, and when he did, each light encountered seemed like a starburst or an elaborate Christmas decoration. Sometimes they reminded him of the artillery shells that had exploded over his head during the Second World War. He and his comrades had watched the bursting shells from what they hoped was the comparative safety of their filthy, water-soaked foxholes. Recently, he had been told that such star-burst lights were common to those who could not see very well, but when he received such information he only nodded thoughtfully. As if such facts might apply to other distant people, but certainly not to him.

Now in the autumn coldness of November, the world was different. The sun would be slow in coming, if it came at all. Sometimes the grey light brought only freezing rain, or stinging sleet. On colder days, the windshield of his truck would be covered with frost and the troublesome muddy ruts of his driveway would be frozen into what seemed like imprecise permanence. Sometimes the tracks of his rubber-soled boots, made in mud and frozen in frost, became almost like works of art, or something akin to the initials that small boys might imprint on still-setting concrete. Created in softness and then stiffened into forms of rigidity.

The deer, when he saw them, had by now exchanged their golden coats of summer sheen for those of autumn grey. Sometimes he saw them at the base of the leafless wild apple trees, nuzzling for the windfalls that had dropped from the bare

3

branches. After heavy winds there would be an abundance of apples on the ground, and the deer would become more selective, taking explorative bites from some and then moving on to others. In later weeks they would eat those they had originally spurned, even those that had rotted or were permanently frozen in the glittering frost.

The rabbits' coats were changing from brown to white, and they were presently in danger from the cruising white-tailed hawks and bald eagles that sometimes ventured inland from the now sullen grey-flecked sea. Field mice were trying to get into his house, where they hoped they might find warmth.

His grey cat purred and curled herself around his ankles. The buzzing of insects now was stilled, and only the hardy purple asters represented the flowers that had once been so prolific. It seemed like a fitting setting for the remembrance of the eleventh hour of the eleventh day of the eleventh month.

Thinking of the asters, he adjusted the plastic poppy pinned to the collar of his blazer. He moved some of the sticks of his woodpile with his toe,

4

looking without urgency for some that might fit into the firebox of his kitchen stove. He knew there was no immediate need for these sticks, as he had a supply of well-measured dry ones neatly stacked behind his stove.

He could smell the smoke from his already lit fire as it wafted forth from his chimney. The smoke comforted him in a way he could not fully understand, as if it had been part of him for as long as he could remember. He recalled that when he was still a small boy he would look at the smoke to make sure of the direction of the wind. If the smoke drifted toward the ocean, the wind would be from the east, and if it slanted a certain way, from the southeast, he knew that this was the direction of the most serious storms. If the smoke was directed inland, the wind would be off the ocean and the waves would be higher, and perhaps more dangerous.

He had heard that, in the suburbs of Montreal, there was a ban against the burning of wood because the odour of woodsmoke annoyed some of the residents. But Montreal was another, mysterious world.

He saw the headlights of the car, piercing the darkness and coming through the trees. He straightened himself into an almost military posture and remained standing, resolutely, near his woodpile.

When the car door opened, the dome light illuminated for a brief instant the elongated form of his grey-haired son who lived on a farm nearby. The man got out of the car with some difficulty. Instead of using his left foot to "set" himself and bear the weight of his body, he first shifted to the edge of the car seat and then stood up. His left foot was encased in an oversized boot, and when he stepped forward to shake his father's hand he did so with a pronounced limp.

"How is your foot?" said his father, his question weighted with concern.

"Not bad," came the answer. "I took some pills. I see you're already dressed. You have your poppy on and everything. Where are your medals?"

"I laid them out on the table for the last time," said his father. "We will wait for a while in the yard."

"Yes," said the younger man. "We'll wait for a while. He'll be along soon. We'll see his headlights coming through the trees. All three of us are early. The ceremony is not until this afternoon."

The grey cat moved toward him.

For some years, David MacDonald had been ambivalent about Remembrance Day. He had been attending the ceremonies for more than fifty years and had outlived all of his comrades. He had visited the schools and marched in the parades. He had ridden on the backs of trucks to the various cenotaphs and participated in the laying of wreaths. In the earlier years there had been some survivors from the First World War and they had always been given the place of honour in the parades. But now they were all gone. Sometimes, he was told, their medals were for sale on eBay. Now there were sometimes younger men, veterans of Korea, or Vietnam, and even, recently, Afghanistan. David MacDonald felt that this would be his last appearance. He smiled at his son in appreciation of his company.

2.

When David MacDonald went to war, it was in 1942 and he was twenty-one years old. He had been married for a year and a half to a girl from a farm two miles away who was sexually precocious. He himself was reserved in that part of life. On their third date, she said, "I'd like to marry a man with a big one, let's see what you've got." He had not expected anything like this to happen at such an early stage in their relationship and was bothered by the fact that he had not changed into clean underwear.

She was the oldest in a family of six girls and it seemed that all of them spoke constantly of the opposite sex. As the oldest, she seemed to feel that it was her duty to marry first and more or less lead the way for her younger sisters. She spoke of "being married" as if it were a job or, perhaps, a place. Sometimes she mentioned Montreal, which was a city she had never visited but where two of her aunts resided. She seemed on a much faster track than he was. He was not opposed to marriage, but questions such as "Where will we live?" "Where will I get a job?" occupied a section of his mind.

After their wedding, they moved in with his austere, widowed father, which they all knew, from the start, was not a good idea. His father was one of those men who were constantly adding up the grocery bills aloud and, in the days before electricity, blowing out the lamps early to save money on kerosene. She thought of his father as a cheap old miser, and his father, in turn, disliked her coming down to breakfast without being fully clothed and revealing, what was, in his opinion, "too much of herself." The couple retreated as often as possible to their bedroom at the head of the stairs.

After the birth of their daughter, the economics of the situation became more and more pronounced. He worked with his father on their small farm and in the woods and in their fishing boat. His father had always allowed him a few dollars when he was a single man but seemed more reluctant to do so now that he was married and a father himself. His wife began to spend more and more time at her parents' loud and jovial house, taking their daughter with her.

It was amid such uncertainty that he enlisted in 1942. He was aware that there were exemptions for married men but also aware that the dependents of married men received cheques from the government. His wife was pregnant again, and although she said she would miss him, she pointed out the advantages of having her own money. They both assumed that the war would not last much longer. It had been going on, after all, for more than three years, and the Dieppe disaster had already taken place.

Still, there was a great deal of patriotic fervour in the air, and the arguments for and against conscription raged continuously. Ration books were coming. He was told that an individual could have either one cup of coffee or one cup of tea in a restaurant but no more. As he seldom went to restaurants, this bit of information did not particularly bother him.

He was also aware that going back as far as the old days in the Scottish Highlands, young men like himself had always gone to war because of their history and their geography but most of all because they were poor.

He went to New Glasgow for basic training, where some made fun of his Gaelic accent. He learned to march in formation, and how to break down and assemble a Bren gun in sixty seconds.

He signed over his pay packet to his wife. They had decided it would be best if she went back to live with her parents. Although it would be overcrowded, she would be more at ease there and her sisters would help with her motherly duties.

Then he went to Halifax, where he had never been before. After that he embarked on an eleven-day crossing to England, landing near Liverpool and being stationed at a basic camp, at Aldershot, in the south. He and his fellow soldiers made one journey to see London, which had been badly bombed, but for the most part they worked within their own parade grounds, rehearsing formations and practising bayonet thrusts into sandbags. The younger soldiers cowered under the barked orders of those in charge. They were told they were being saved for an important mission. This important mission proved to be the front lines of Ortona, Italy, where the Germans had been established for some time.

In remembrance, all of his senses still seemed rawly open to those scenes of mud and desolation from that time of more than fifty years ago; the month-long campaign in the cold, rain-darkened days of December; the earth-shaking artillery explosions and the hurtling shards of shrapnel; the mounting losses of men around him from wounds or illness, so bad that young soldiers who barely knew how to fire a gun were thrown into action; some of the young boys weeping and soiling themselves; officers, or the sergeants who replaced them, urging their men on toward the next German-occupied ruined house; the houses with terrified Italian men, women, and children hiding in the cellars; the tiny allocations of rum.

He remembered that sometimes during the lulls they were sent to retrieve the bodies of those who had fallen in previous forays. If the bodies had been exposed for some time they were blackened and bloated and seemed ready to explode. When they were rolled over to be placed on the blanket stretchers, the odour was overpowering.

He remembered that what had bothered him most was not being able to offer any help to those who were still alive but doomed to certain death: the young man with his fingers linked across his stomach, desperately trying to hold in his intestines, even as the light faded from his eyes; the young man without legs, rolling sideways as bloody spittle bubbled from his lips.

He remembered that it was there that a screaming wounded man, left at night between the lines, was put out of his misery when a Canadian crawled out to end it with a knife to the throat, not knowing in the dark if he was dealing with friend or foe.

He remembered, too, that when it was all over, the small town of shattered stone houses had been taken after one week at the price of two thousand Canadians dead.

Later, when they were shipped to northeastern Holland, it was April. In the little port of Delfzijl, across from the German city of Emden, shells rained down from entrenchments on the dikes. Still, it was said the Germans were in disarray, although it did not seem much like it until their defensive ring was finally broken on the first of May. Rumours swirled about the war's end, and then on May 5 it was official. The Germans had surrendered, Holland was liberated, the war in Europe was over.

The Canadians began to push southbound toward the city of Groningen, taking prisoners on their way. He remembered three distinct groups of people from those days: the Germans who had surrendered, some, it seemed, in relief, while others were sullen and snarled at their captors. Many of them were young and willingly accepted offerings of cigarettes and chocolate.

The second group consisted of the freed prisoners. When the prisons were opened, the emaciated figures spilled forth shouting, "Tommy, Tommy," because the helmets the Canadians wore were modelled on those of the British. They clutched the sleeves of their liberators with skeletal fingers. Many of them were no more than skin and bones, he remembered.

And then there were the Dutch themselves. Many of the men were old, as the younger men had been forced into labour camps and some sent to Germany itself. The women and children wept and kissed the Canadian soldiers. Little girls offered tin cans containing flowers. Orange banners flapped in the wind and "Thank you, Canada" was painted on the roofs of the barns. The church bells had been silenced during all the years of war, but on May 5 the first music that rang out from the Groningen cathedral was "O Canada!"

Still, the country was a disaster. The people had come through "The Hungry Winter," many of them subsisting on only sugar beets and flower bulbs. Their country, which had hoped to remain neutral, had been occupied for five long years and was now reduced to soggy ruins. Dead cattle lay rotting by the roadsides. He remembered the smell as he and the soldiers pushed south.

Although the war was officially over, the machinery for getting the men home to Canada moved slowly. American soldiers were given first preference in terms of transatlantic crossing and then those Canadians who had enlisted first. It was a lengthy process. During the summer of 1945, there were one hundred and seventy thousand Canadian soldiers in Holland, and by the end of November there were still seventy thousand there. Many of them were billeted in private homes.

While he was away, from 1942 through 1945, the letters from his wife had become increasingly infrequent. They were written, he realized, by someone else, probably one of her younger sisters. He had never considered whether his wife was literate. They had been so consumed with each other physically that there had not seemed much time for anything else. In retrospect, he realized he had never seen her reading the *Family Herald* (which was the only newspaper to which his father subscribed) before the lamp was blown out. The letters that he did receive contained little information, mostly descriptions of the weather in far-off Nova Scotia.

When his troop ship finally landed in Halifax, it was snowing. He and most of the others were still in full uniform. On the dock a fellow soldier offered to sell him an army rifle that he had smuggled across the ocean in his duffle bag. He had sawed off part of the barrel so it would fit into the bag and then reattached the front sights to the shortened barrel. He also had a few shells, which he threw in as part of the bargain. The price of the transaction was a dollar.

Later, on the overcrowded train to northeastern Nova Scotia, there was a great deal of raucous celebration. Men drank openly from their brown-bagged bottles and sang off-colour songs. Mothers tried to cover their young children's ears. A soldier stood in the aisle with a baseball bat he had borrowed from one of the children while a friend pitched oranges to him. When the bat made contact, the oranges exploded, spraying the passengers with juice and seeds and mushy pulp. Through all this some people slept and dreamed, and froth bubbled from their lips.

When he finally arrived, he went first to his in-laws' house, where he assumed his wife was staying. The house was hot and overcrowded and filled with women. His father-in-law had died during the previous winter, but no one had informed him. He hugged both of his daughters, one of whom had not been born when he had enlisted. From an adjoining room his wife brought forth an energetic little boy. "This is another David MacDonald," she said. "Say hello to Daddy."

The child, clearly under two years old, ran forward and hugged his brown-serged pantleg as if he had been rehearsing.

The room lapsed into silence. He sat down, and the child sat on his lap and played with the buttons on his tunic.

From the start, the child showed a fierce affection for him. He was later to think that perhaps he was a sort of novelty as a masculine presence in a house of so many women, but he could not be sure. For a brief time he thought that his in-laws were encouraging the child to win over his affections, but he soon realized that could not be true. The child was too young, and his in-laws were not given to that sort of planned deception.

He went to visit his own father, whom he found as austere as ever. "Well, what do you think?" asked his father.

"Not much," he said, trying to sound as non-committal as he could. He felt somehow that he should defend his wife against his father's stern morality, but he was not sure of that either.

When he first lay with his wife, he was hesitant and uncertain. He remembered that, in the barracks, soldiers had said that certain Arab or African men would not sleep with their wives if they knew their wives had experienced sexual relations with men other than themselves. He was not sure if this were true, or if it mattered. He realized that a lot of the talk in the barracks bordered on the fantastical and was little more than nonsense. Still, he wondered if such talk was having an effect upon him or if it was just his own personal situation. He wondered if he would be the same had he never heard such talk and never encountered what he had.

Too late for that.

"I couldn't do without it," his wife said. "I bet you sowed a lot of your seed in Holland and Europe and all those other places." He was surprised at her use of the phrase "sowed a lot of your seed" and realized how very little he really knew her.

They had been in a married relationship for just over a year and he was not sure if he had changed or she had changed, or if it was the circumstances that surrounded them. Things did not go well under such circumstances.

For a year and a half he worked with his father cutting pit timbers for the nearby mine. Sometimes he slept at his in-laws' house and sometimes at his father's. His daughters enjoyed the attention lavished upon them by their young aunts, who were constantly arranging their hair, experimenting with lipstick and nail polish, or admiring the dress styles of the models in the Eaton's catalogue. They showed no interest in their other, glum grandfather and relatively little in him.

The young David MacDonald, however, was different. He burst into smiles whenever he saw him and tried to follow him everywhere. Sometimes when he visited his in-laws, he could see the child waiting at the window as if he had been anticipating him for a long time.

One winter evening he left the house of his in-laws to take his father's horses back to their home barn. It was cold and the horses snorted and tossed their heads impatiently as they cantered along the snow-covered road. After they reached the barn, he took his time unharnessing the horses and putting hay in their mangers. As he was leaving the stable, he became aware of movement beneath the horse robes in the back of the sleigh. He discovered the child, who extended his arms so he could be lifted from the sleigh. He wore only a light shirt and trousers and was blue with the cold. There was frost on his eyelashes and his cheeks were chilled by frozen tears. He threw his icy arms around his discoverer's neck and pressed his cold cheek against neglected whiskers.

That night when they were preparing for bed, he noticed that the child wore no underwear and was still shivering. He draped one of his flannel shirts upon the child's small frame and inserted the slender arms into the shirt's sleeves. The shirt hung down beneath the boy's knees like the smock of an ancient monk. Later he wakened to the embrace of small arms around his neck and the pulsing body heat that emanated through the flannel and seemed to fuse their bodies closer together.

It went on for another year. The mine was in

trouble and the market for pit timbers declined. Sometimes he and his father cut fence posts for the bigger farm owners, but there was little predictable income in that. He did not wish to stay with his wife's family, nor she under the scrutiny of his father. At one time they had planned to start a house of their own, but their limited enthusiasm for such a venture had now completely dissipated.

Many of the younger veterans with whom he marched in the Legion parades began to drift off to southern Ontario, to the car plants in Windsor, to Polymer in Sarnia, to Massey Ferguson in Brantford, to Continental Can in Toronto. One day his wife announced that she was going to Montreal to work for a while in a garment factory. Her aunts had found her a job. She would send some money to help support the children.

The children seemed mainly unaffected by her absence. The girls continued to dress up and explore new hairstyles with their young aunts while David MacDonald spent more and more time with the older men he seemed to have chosen. He began to imitate the manner of their walking and their speech patterns, including their comments on the weather. As his sisters seemed destined to be forever young, so he seemed to be headed in the opposite direction and to willingly embrace an advanced maturity far beyond the years of his chronological age.

It was a late November evening that he came breathlessly to their door. He had taken a shortcut through the woods and across the swamp, which was now frozen because of the season. He wore no jacket but only a thin, faded plaid shirt.

"They've come to get me," he said as if he were announcing the arrival of abducting aliens.

"Who?" said David MacDonald.

"My mom," he said, "and a man who is with her. They want to take us all to Montreal."

"Well, we'll have to talk about it," said David MacDonald, himself in a state of confusion.

"There is a car coming," said his austere father. "I see the headlights through the trees."

"It's them," said the child, bolting for the door.

"Wait a minute," said David MacDonald, seizing the shoulder of the faded shirt, which ripped and came apart in his grasping hand. The child fled into the descending darkness, slamming the door behind him.

They went outside.

The car came up the driveway, its headlights illuminating the frozen ruts over which its suspension bounced. There was a man at the wheel and David MacDonald's wife sat in the passenger seat beside him. The two excited girls were in the back seat amid a clutter of shopping bags that spilled an assortment of clean and unclean clothing across the seat and onto the floor.

"Where is he?" she said. "It's getting dark and we're in a hurry. Jacques says we've got to get into New Brunswick before midnight."

His father went inside to get the lantern, and all of them, except the man behind the wheel, called the child's name, which seemed to vanish on the rising wind. It was beginning to snow.

They followed the austere, lantern-carrying father into the barn, still calling the child's name. On the threshing floor there was a ladder that led up to the hayloft, where the grey cat kept her kittens secreted within a hole in the sheltering hay. Because he carried the light, the austere father was able to see and reached the threshing floor first. He knocked the ladder flat and kicked some hay over it before the others followed him into the dimly lit space.

They kept calling the child's name.

"David, David," they called, but there was no sound from the muffled hay, only the impatient animals shifting in their stalls.

"We've got to get going," said David MacDonald's wife. "Jacques says we've got to get into New Brunswick before it gets much later. It's beginning to snow. I'll let you know when we get back to Montreal and we can make arrangements."

They left the barn and went back into the yard. Jacques was drumming his fingers impatiently on the steering wheel.

"Do you want to be doing this?" said David MacDonald to his flesh-and-blood daughters, who, after the search, had returned to the chaos of the back seat.

"Yes," they said. "It will be fun. Montreal has street lights and lots of restaurants. There is a merry-go-round not far from where Mom lives."

None of them ever reached Montreal, nor for that matter the New Brunswick border. All of them were killed when their car collided with a transport truck on the narrow wooden bridge outside of Tatamagouche, on the "Sunrise Trail." It was near midnight and snowing quite heavily and the roads were slippery and the visibility poor. Perhaps Jacques was tired or unfamiliar with the narrow roads. It was said that when the occupants spilled from the car, the wife of David MacDonald and her oldest daughter were still alive, but it was snowing and dark and isolated and by the time help arrived it was too late. Jacques, it was learned, worked in the laundry room of the Ritz-Carlton hotel in Montreal. All of this information did not reach them until the following day. They had no telephone and the neighbours' lines had been blown down by the storm.

After the car with the Quebec plates left the yard, they stood for a while and watched the red tail lights vanish into the enveloping snow and then they went inside where it was, at least, warmer. After a while the austere father said, "You better go out to the barn and put the ladder up to the hayloft."

"Why?" said David MacDonald, who was still in a state of confusion.

"You'll see," said his father, who rose to put a stick in the fire.

David MacDonald took the lantern and went out to the barn. He found the ladder partly covered in hay and placed it against the loft and then went back inside.

A short time later the child came through the door. The shoulder of his shirt was torn and wisps of hay clung to his clothes and to his hair. He had a blue plastic bowl in his hand.

"How is the grey cat and her kittens?" said David MacDonald's father.

"She's fine," said the child. "I'm going to get her some milk. I don't want to go back to Mom's," he continued. "I'm afraid they'll come back and take me. Can I stay here?"

"You don't have to go back," said David MacDonald's father. "You can stay here. We will leave the cat's milk until the morning. It is too dark to climb the ladder now. You should go to bed. You can sleep with your father."

David MacDonald was surprised to hear himself described to the child as "your father," but now and in the weeks and months that followed there seemed no way of avoiding it. Perhaps his father had not liked his wife, but he clearly bore no animosity toward her child. The weeks and months stretched into years, and when the boy went to the Co-op to pick up feed or farm equipment, he signed the bills or receipts as "David MacDonald," which was, after all, his given name. He was tremendously good with animals and had a calming effect upon them. Mothers giving birth allowed him to stroke their heads, and strange dogs never barked or growled in his presence but moved toward him to lick his hand.

In the afternoon of November 11, 1952, the two David MacDonalds were filleting mackerel out in the yard. The elder one had returned from the Remembrance Day ceremonies and they were preparing the fish so that they might have them for food during the coming winter months. Later they would pack them in buckets, alternating layers of mackerel with layers of salt.

They looked up from their work to see a magnificent buck grazing in the field beyond them. Because their thoughts were on food and because they knew the meat would not spoil in the cooler days of autumn, they decided to act. Silently the boy entered the house and returned with a knife, four bullets, and the sawed-off rifle that had seen action in Holland.

David MacDonald lay down on his stomach and inched forward through the dying grass, propelling himself on his elbows and loading the rifle as he moved. His hands were still bloody and greasy from handling the entrails of the mackerel, and the worn grass tickled his neck and pressed against his chest and stomach in a manner that reminded him of Ortona. The boy crouched close behind him with the knife. The buck lifted his head and sniffed the wind. The wind was from the south and his stalkers were crawling from the north. He lowered his head and continued to graze.

It all happened in a matter of seconds. David MacDonald rose up as he had been taught, firing his rifle as he came to his knees in a single, fluid military motion. The buck collapsed and then leapt to his feet. David MacDonald realized that because the barrel of the rifle had been shortened, the sights were misaligned and he hastened to reload, his fingers still slippery from the fish. He fired again. He heard the boy scream as he fell before him. In the field beyond, the buck had collapsed again and now lay still. The knife fell from the boy's hand as he tried to staunch the blood and slivers of bone that pulsed from his shattered ankle.

After the first shot, the boy had leapt forward

with his knife to bleed the animal without realizing that a second shot was coming. David MacDonald fashioned a tourniquet out of his shirt and belt as he had been taught in the army and tightened it with the knife. Beyond them the silent body of the buck began to fill with its own gases and lay like the bloated cattle near the ruined roadways of Holland.

They were in trouble. If they went immediately to the hospital, the authorities would have to report the gunshot wound to the police. The gun was illegal. They had no permit, and they had no hunting licence, and the body of the buck lay heavy and obvious before them. Blood spurted from the boy's ankle whenever the tourniquet was loosened.

David MacDonald was to wonder for the rest of his life whether the delay before they went to the hospital, without legal repercussions, resulted in the boy being permanently crippled, although the medical authorities said it was not so.

"Maybe," he said to the boy later, "I ruined your life."

"Maybe," said the boy, "you saved it."

"I should never have brought that rifle home from the war," said David MacDonald, "but then I guess a lot happened because of the war."

4.

As I begin to tell this, it is November 11, Remembrance Day, I am on a gravel road that leads to my grandfather's house in rural Cape Breton. It is early in the morning and I have been driving for four hours in my rental car from the Halifax International Airport. Driving in the dark for four hours by yourself on Remembrance Day is a certain kind of experience, making you think of how the present always comes out of the past.

There are few distractions and relatively few vehicles on the major highway. As you penetrate deeper into Cape Breton, traffic is even further reduced, but you have to be aware of animals lurking by the roadside or emerging from the ditches. Their eyes glow in the headlights' beams. They are going about their nocturnal business: foxes, coyotes, raccoons, wildcats, bears, deer, even moose. There are no porcupines, nor skunks, on Cape Breton Island, or as one wag said in reference to skunks: "No four-legged ones!"

I will never encounter any of these animals with their glowing eyes in the practice of my professional life. They will never be anesthetized upon my operating table.

My name is David MacDonald, and the men to whom I travel are called David MacDonald as well. I am a veterinarian and, it seems, by most standards, a reasonably successful one. I specialize now in "small animals," although it was not always so. I have three clinics located in the suburbs of Toronto, Canada's largest city. Much of my work involves the spaying and neutering of dogs and cats. The fee for a dog's castration is $250 and most owners do not seem to mind. There is also a great demand for the declawing of cats so they will not damage their owners' expensive urban furniture. You may have seen my billboards along the major highways, or my elaborate ads in the Yellow Pages. They proclaim: "For a healthy pet, see your vet." On the left-hand side of the advertisements is my name, "David MacDonald, D.V.M.," and then those of my associates. In the upper-right-hand corner there is a family of five happy kittens. In the middle, there is a list of the services we offer. Besides the neutering and declawing, we specialize in Heartworm and Flea Protection, Dentistry, Grooming, Endoscopy, Surgery, Nutritional Counselling, etc. There is a growth in "nutritional counselling" because many modern pets suffer from obesity due to lack of exercise. Lack of exercise is not a concern for the animals whose eyes gleam in my headlights. Sometimes the fat female cats are simply pregnant and their owners do not know "how it happened." "Well, it won't happen again," they say resolutely. "Can I make an appointment?"

"What will I do with the kittens?" some of them ask.

"After about three to four weeks, after their eyes

are open, you might try the pet shops or the Humane Society," I say. I realize that ads offering "free kittens to a good home" seldom work anymore.

And I know also that the pet shops and even the Humane Society are reluctant to take kittens, especially if they are black. There is more of a chance should the kittens be calico or tortoiseshell. I can usually tell which of the clients in my office will try very hard for the placement of such kittens. Our clinics do euthanasia as well.

We are planning to expand our business to include the sale of pet supplies: dishes and baskets, and bowls and beds, and monograms and grave markers and even puppy pyjamas. Although some kittens are euthanized, some "teacup dogs" are valued at $40,000. There is a great love out there for life of the right kind, and for some, great care is given.

I pull to the side of the gravel road and stand to urinate. In the darkness of the early morning, the sky is beginning to lighten. There are no headlights approaching from either direction. The coyote pack yips to the north. I am only a mile from my grandfather's house, and although it is still dark, I imagine that the men to whom I travel are already standing in the yard. They are always up early, although there is no need.

Perhaps they are up early because of a habit instilled in them by an even older man, a man whom I never saw but who exists in remembrance with the adjective "austere" attached to him. He was my grandfather's father and apparently died in the same bed in which he was born and probably conceived. Although he was austere, both of the men to whom I travel maintain that he "saved" them, each in his way, and in so doing probably saved me as well, although I was far distant in his future. He apparently used to say to them that no one who was in bed after seven in the morning amounted to anything. This may be questionable, but all of us are early risers.

They will see the headlights coming through the trees. They will be standing side by side as they have supported each other for more than half a century. One man near ninety and the other in his late sixties. They are like two adjacent trees that do not touch but share the same root system, although I must admit that this analogy goes a bit too far.

Once, the older man shot the other in the ankle, rendering him permanently crippled and thus altering the path and direction of his life. It all came about directly or indirectly because of the war, which we are commemorating today. This is the older man's last Remembrance Day where he will be standing straight and trim in his blue blazer, with his poppy firmly affixed, and his beret worn at a certain, almost rakish, angle. His eyesight is failing and his driving is erratic. Seventy years ago, in a time no one but himself remembers, he was a young man, driven energetically by sexual desire, who joined the army because of poverty and the opportunity to serve his country. And, indeed, "the war changed everything."

My name is David MacDonald, and I am here at the request of my father, whose name is also David MacDonald and who was once shot by the older man, whose name is David MacDonald as well. We are all part of history and "how the war changed everything," and how this time came out of that time.

An hour ago, I passed the sleeping and prosperous dairy farm established by my other grandparents. It was still in darkness, its silos rising like confident monuments to modern-day agriculture. These grandparents are gone now, but I will see some of their descendants later at the cenotaph. They were Dutch, and their daughter, my mother, married my father when she was a young girl barely out of her teens.

After the war, Holland was a disaster and the Dutch government encouraged many of its young people to emigrate because it did not know what to do with them. Canada, because of "the liberation," was "a friend," and there were opportunities in the new country that did not exist in the old.

The Dutch came by the thousands, many of them to Nova Scotia. Because a number of them were basically agricultural people, they purchased and settled on farms that were at first viewed as marginal or non-productive. My MacDonald grandfather jokes that after he liberated the Dutch, the Dutch followed him to Nova Scotia. The Nova Scotia government advanced loans to thousands of potential farmers so that they might establish themselves with machinery and seed for crops and the necessary animals. By the time the loans were due, all but one family had paid them off entirely.

The part about the loans was told to me by my Dutch relatives, so perhaps we are just trying to gild our own lilies. I have often wondered though about "the one family." No one seems to know where this "one family" lived, so perhaps it is similar to the Dutch supposedly having nine words for clean, although no one seems able to recite all of them.

My Dutch grandfather once told me that during the dark days of the German occupation, a young girl who was his relative was "keeping company" with a young German soldier. Her family was in the underground resistance, and her grandfather kept a scribbler with the names and addresses of his fellow resisters in a drawer beneath his socks and underwear. She had often seen the scribbler but, in the manner of the young, paid little attention to it. One day in a discussion with her young man, the subject of the scribbler came up. He asked her if she could get him the scribbler and in return he would give her a tiny radio that played all the current pop songs. She agreed to the bargain. Most of the people whose names were in the scribbler were lined up and shot, including some members of her immediate family. The people were shot early in the morning when most of them were still in their nightclothes.

The soldiers never came for my grandparents. No one knows why. Perhaps the soldiers had other things to do. Perhaps they ran out of bullets. Perhaps that particular page of the scribbler was torn out. Perhaps they turned two pages at once. Perhaps the scribbler itself was lost and trampled in the mud beneath muddy boots. It all seemed based on the fickleness of chance and the desperation of those caught up in the war.

After the Liberation, the girl's hair was cut off because she had been a collaborator, but her life was spared because it was felt she had suffered — and would suffer — enough. She, too, apparently came to Canada and blended in with the Dutch families in Ontario. Her descendants raise flowers for the large urban markets of southern Ontario. We all make mistakes, especially during war.

Because my father was permanently maimed, he became, in his small community, a figure of some sympathy and the recipient of "a government job." The job, with the Department of Highways, was running the road grader in summer and the snowplow in winter.

It was traditional at this time that if there was a change of government, all the employees of the defeated government would be fired and replaced by those from the winning side. My father, however, was more or less "left alone," and considered himself fortunate for most of his working life.

One winter his snowplow went off the road in a blinding blizzard. Prior to the event, he had been almost frozen, protected in his cab by only a thin sheet of plastic. He had found it necessary to urinate on his hands so that he might restore some warmth and movement in his fingers, in order to handle his controls. After the accident, he limped toward the nearest light. Inside the house was a family of Dutch immigrants, including my mother. The house was warm and sparkling in its cleanliness. At this time, he and David MacDonald were living alone, dining on potatoes and salt pork or fish, with occasionally a can of beans. He was amazed at the difference in lives and at the possibilities that lay before him.

I am thinking of this as I stand by the road.

Everything going back to the war.

In the darkness of this Remembrance Day I will go to stand with the David MacDonalds. First, they will see the headlights of my car coming though the trees. All three of us up too early for the day that lies ahead. I will smile when my grandfather embraces me and says, "Thank you for coming." Sometimes he adds, with a smile, "We vets have to stick together." He knows it's a bad joke but likes the punning repetition.

He sees me, as I see myself, as a link in a chain reaching back to the Second World War and to its aftermath. "He has never denied his love," says my father, "and we will remember that." I do not know the intimacies of their lives, only what I have been told. But sometimes in Toronto, I lay aside the *Journal of the American Veterinary Medical Association* and put on hold my possible expansion into the world of puppy pyjamas. And there comes to me the image of my father as a small chilled child, without underwear, laying his tear-stained cheeks against the icy whiskers of the man he worshipped as his father.

I do not know who my father's biological father

was, and I do not know if even the senior David MacDonald knows. Perhaps the information died with my grandmother and her two daughters, who were my aunts. All of them splayed out on the highway at the wooden bridge near Tatamagouche. Never to make it to the New Brunswick border, nor to Montreal, where there were reported to be merry-go-rounds. Perhaps the young woman who was my grandmother was not only sexually enthusiastic but also hopeful of leaving behind what she perceived as poverty, and hopeful of starting a new life beyond the New Brunswick border. Because she was in a hurry to get on with her life, she left one of her children behind in the barn.

The senior David MacDonald told me that he and his fellow soldiers once made a return visit to the Holland they had liberated years before. They were in their blazers and berets with their medals on their chests. They were older men but still able to march in formation. The Dutch lined both sides of the streets and applauded them. He said that in Apeldoorn, among the congratulatory signs, he first noticed signs of a different nature. They were held up by middle-aged people and were directed at the Canadian soldiers. They asked a simple question, "Are you my father?" In 1946, it was reported that there were seven thousand children born of Canadian soldiers who were once billeted in the Netherlands. These children, too, had, in their way, been left behind by young men who were eager to get on with their lives. Most of the old men were in marching formation and directed their eyes straight ahead.

I put my car in gear and drive toward the waiting men. They will see my headlights coming through the trees. All of us are early on this Remembrance Day. All of our lives were affected by a war that brought its changes down upon us. Some of us were saved by actions, and some by accident, as the past produced the present.

I feel and hear the gravel turn as I drive toward the light. I go to stand and take my place within the continuum of time.

A Note on the Text

Remembrance is an original story commissioned from the
author by the Vancouver Writers Fest, and released as a
limited edition chapbook in 2012, to commemorate the
festival's twenty-fifth anniversary. Acknowledgement is
made to Doug Gibson, for his insightful editorial help
and support. And to Hal Wake, Artistic Director of the
Vancouver Writers Fest.

In 2013, the story appeared as a Hazlitt Original e-book,
published by McClelland & Stewart.

Remembrance is Alistair MacLeod's last published story.
It appears for the first time in book form in this edition.

About the Author

Alistair MacLeod was born in North Battleford,
Saskatchewan, and raised among an extended family
in Cape Breton, Nova Scotia. MacLeod's only novel,
No Great Mischief, won numerous awards, including
the International IMPAC Dublin Literary Award, the
Dartmouth Book Award for Fiction, the Thomas Raddall
Atlantic Fiction Award, and the Trillium Book Award.
He was also the author of two internationally acclaimed
collections of short stories: *The Lost Salt Gift of Blood*
and *As Birds Bring Forth the Sun*. In 2000, these two books,
accompanied by previously unpublished stories, were
brought together in a single-volume edition entitled
Island: The Collected Stories.

Alistair MacLeod died in April 2014.